Megan's
Tick Tock
Rocket

First published 2007
Evans Brothers Limited
2A Portman Mansions
Chiltern Street
London W1U 6NR

British Library Cataloguing in Publication Data

Peters, Andrew (Andrew Fusek)
    Megan's tick tock rocket. - (Spirals)
    1. Children's stories
    I. Title II. Peters, Polly
    823.9'14[J]

ISBN-10: 0 237 53348 0 (hb)
ISBN-13: 978 0 237 53348 9 (hb)

ISBN-10: 0 237 53342 1 (pb)
ISBN-13: 978 0 237 53342 7 (pb)

Printed in China

Series Editor: Nick Turpin
Design: Robert Walster
Production: Jenny Mulvanny

Megan's Tick Tock Rocket

Andrew Fusek Peters, Polly Peters and Simona Dimitri

Megan found most days a bore
Everything was such a chore!
She hated tidying things away

Or shopping when
she longed to play.

Making beds took far too long
And sitting still to work felt wrong.
Even meal times seemed to last
Forever, creeping slowly past.

7

"Right!" said Megan. "Time for action!
I'll build myself a fine contraption.
It will be a grand machine
That plays with time like plasticine!"

It only took an hour to make,
With cogs and wheels and a garden rake,
A cardboard box, a broken clock,
Elastic bands and one red sock.

"Yippee! I'm ready!" Megan cried,
And straight away she hopped inside
And pressed the button: off she roared,
Far away from feeling bored!

13

"How amazing! How fantastic!
My machine makes time elastic!"
So, off she zipped around the park,
Stretching out the hours 'til dark.

She saw the clock hands spinning past
And hours speeding super fast.
"Hooray! Now, time won't drag for me,
My tick tock rocket sets me free!

Far up above her rose the moon
"Watch out!" cried Megan.
Zip-Zap-Zoooom!
"Why stay here to simply play
When I could tour the Milky Way?"

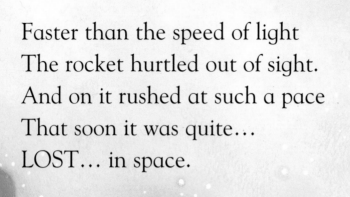

Faster than the speed of light
The rocket hurtled out of sight.
And on it rushed at such a pace
That soon it was quite...
LOST... in space.

"Oh dear," sniffed Megan, "Just my luck,
my great idea has come unstuck."
But worse, a sudden CRACK! And POP!
Brought Megan's rocket to a STOP.

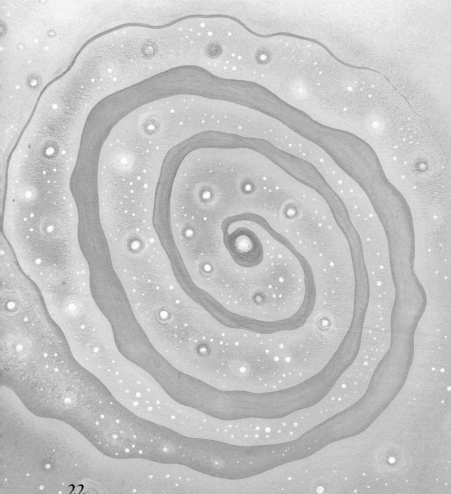

So there she sat, quite still for hours
Just watching endless meteor showers.
This was boring, lonely too:
She wished she had some chores to do!

Could Megan mend her tick tock rocket?
She pulled out what was in her pocket:
A paperclip, a peg, a purse –
And made a lever, marked **Reverse**.

Back through time she swiftly sped
And landed on her own dear bed!
She had escaped eternity
And made it home in time for tea.

Next day, the hours still dragged by
But did she grumble, did she sigh?
No, not at all, while back at home
She tidied up without a moan…
Later, in the park she played
Until the day filled up with shade.

And as for Megan's tick-tock rocket?
It's in the cupboard. Time to lock it!

Why not try reading a Spirals book?

Megan's Tick Tock Rocket by Andrew Fusek Peters,
Polly Peters, and Simona Dimitri
ISBN 978 0237 53342 7

Growl! by Vivian French and Tim Archbold
ISBN 978 0237 53345 8

John and the River Monster by Paul Harrison and Ian
Benfold Haywood
ISBN 978 0237 53344 1

Froggy Went a Hopping by Alan Durant and Sue Mason
ISBN 978 0237 53346 5